Lord Lister, known as Raffles, Master Thief

by Kurt Matull and Theo Blankensee

translated by Joseph A. Lovece

Dime Novel Cover Vol. 8

Also by the author:

The Steam Man of the West
The Road Home
The Flying Prairie Schooner
The Transatlantic Race

Dime Novel Cover:

Denver Doll the Detective Queen
Six Weeks in the Moon
Hank Hound, the Crescent City Detective
Sherlock Holmes Versus Jack the Ripper
Hercules, the Dumb Destroyer
Night Hawk
Sexton Blake: The Missing Millionaire

TABLE OF CONTENTS

Introduction………………..………………………………1

Lord Lister……....………………………………………..4

Cover Gallery……………….………………………….92

Introduction

Between 1908 and 1968 around 300 stories of Lord
Lister, known as Raffles, Master Thief have been translated into
or written in Danish, Dutch, German, Indonesian, Italian, Polish,
Portuguese, Russian, Spanish, Swedish and Turkish. But never
English.

And that's not only inconceivable but also a shame
because the character, sometimes described as Europe's greatest
pulp hero, and his stories are great fun.

Lord Lister aka Raffles was created for publisher Verlag
Gustav Müller & Co. in Berlin by Kurt Matull and Theo
Blankensee (or van Blankensee) exploiting E.W. Hornung's
popular character A.J. Raffles. Matull was a a German writer and
film producer and director. Among other jobs, from 1902-1906
he worked for New York's Evening Post newspaper's editorial
staff. He also wrote or translated Nick Carter stories. Blankensee
is best known today for writing the German Sherlock Holmes

1

pastiche dime novels (see *Dime Novel Cover No. 4, Sherlock Holmes Versus Jack the Ripper*). Together they're credited with 110 Lord Lister novels.

Going forward after the original run ended Robert Hans van Gulik (creator of Judge Dee) wrote about a dozen sequels in Dutch. Felix Hageman wrote an additional 198 stories. That series continued to January 1968.

John C. Raffles is a quintessential Robin Hood character. "A year ago I became Raffles to balance the wealthy and starving classes," he tells his friend and Secretary Charlie Brand. He also informs him that he chose his path since being a master thief is much more challenging than being a detective. He notes: "After carefully considering the matter I came to the conclusion that if one want to use crime as sport, it would mean that it would be more interesting to be the prey than the hunter, or better put to be the criminal instead of the detective.

And he's well-equipped for the job. He tells his foil the bumbling Police Inspector Baxter that he is an expert shot, boxer and fencer, the best at his club. He has ample opportunity to show his prowess, and in one scene uses jiu-jitsu to easily defeat a dangerous criminal who is outraged by Lister's Zen-like carriage.

Throughout the well-written story is a well-developed sense of humor, as the protagonist ceaselessly taunts Scotland Yard, including warning them about his next operation, much to the amusement of one of his pursuers, Detective Marholm, who is depicted as the most capable of Scotland Yard's detective. Indeed, it reminds one of the classic Hollywood screwball comedies.

Even Sherlock Holmes, mentioned several times in the first story, manages to evoke some laugh-out loud humor. In the short novel a letter from Britain's most famous detective informs Scotland Yard that he is enjoying Raffles's antics so much, that he declines their request to help catch him. "'That is,' said Sergeant Tyler, 'what Sherlock Holmes enjoys about Scotland Yard and he wants to show us that perhaps we can catch flies without him, but not criminals.'"

For these reasons it is an honor to be able to introduce Lord Lister, known as Raffles, Master Thief to an English-speaking audience.

Modern German publishers have far outstripped Americans in reprinting their rare old dime novels and several of his stories are available in facsimile editions, for those so inclined to read more.

As a bonus, for this edition also included is a cover gallery depicting a sample of some of the magazine's iterations, in various languages.

Chapter I

Following Innocence

It was six o'clock in the afternoon when the rich silk importer Lucas Brown was about to inform his accountant to close for the business day.

Mr. Brown went to the establishment's broad window overlooking London's Strand, and basking by the closed store's Indian artifacts watched the hustle and bustle of the big city.

Before the accountant left his private office after being informed it was closing time, Mr. Brown said to him:

"Send in the new recruit, Miss Walton, for her interview."

The accountant bowed and hid an ironic smile. He knew his boss and knew what he meant.

Mr. Brown preferred young and inexperienced women, whose appearance appealed to him.

"Absolutely," he replied, "she will fulfill her duties to your complete satisfaction."

"Excellent," said Mr. Brown, rubbing his fleshy hands, "I'm glad to hear it! She's very nice. When I entertain a girl it boosts her career."

The accountant bowed again to conceal his smile.

Outside the room he hear could hear newsboys ringing out, hawking the latest evening newspapers, and the leading sensation the sheets contained:

"Raffles strikes again!" they yelled. "Raffles, the Great Unknown, robbed a quarter of a million in jewels! Raffles! Raffles! Raffles is nowhere to be found!"

Mr. Brown watched, as the passers-by tore up the sheets of newsprint.

"I'm going to start an evening newspaper!" he said to his accountant, "this Raffles is a great attraction."

The accountant disappeared and after a few minutes procured the desired newspaper which offered up in large font Raffles' latest crimes.

Mr. Brown hastily flew over the article and said to his accountant:

"Quite an incredible man. It's unprecedented! With uncanny refinement his work has kept our entire judicial system jumping. And they have yet to find so much as a trouser button! Sherlock Holmes is nowhere to be seen. Without him our vaunted Scotland Yard has turned into a ladies sewing circle."

5

"Well," said the accountant, "this Raffles is a genie. I must confess, the man is impressive! He must have a really unusual talent. He is the king of thieves. A Napoleon! In addition, he is unquestionably a gentleman!"

"I think you're all are crazy, my dear sir. Raffles fever has gripped London. Wherever you go, the Gentleman Thief is all they talk about. A lovely gentleman!" Mr. Brown puckered his fat lips contemptuously. "They seem to have a strange view of him."

"Not at all, Mr. Brown," replied the accountant. "It's a fact that whatever this unknown burglar steals benefits the poor in Whitechapel and East End."

"The man is despicable," said Mr. Brown excitedly. "Complete rubbish! He would do better if he used what he steals for decent purposes. He should do it for wine, women and song. These peasants in Whitechapel and East End would not get a penny from me."

"All right," said the accountant, dropping his smile, "that's exactly what concerns Raffles. Instead of the pennies you won't give the poor he takes the pound notes from your pocket. This is more profitable."

Brown knitted his eyebrows together over his angry little eyes and said, quite irritated: "You go too far, Mr. Thomas. Please refrain from speaking about my money with such familiarity. If you weren't such a longtime and faithful officer I would resent what you just said.

"About—puh!—let's not fight over Raffles. The main thing is that he has gotten away unscathed stealing other people's money rather than mine."

"Let's hope for the best. I don't think you have so much that he would pay you a visit," said the accountant.

"What?" yelled Mr. Brown, "I don't have enough? grrrr. I'm a millionaire! I am a supplier to the English Court! I'm the tip-top!"

"So much the better for Raffles when he comes!"

"Be quiet, you're making me nervous. From your speeches you would believe he is already behind you and invisible."

The accountant laughed: "Since he has manners, poor people help him so it would be an uncomfortable night if he were invisibly trying to take pound notes from your pocket. He may jump out of your coffee, Mr. Brown."

Just then he raised his short, broad and angry figure and called out: "Stop with your stupid jokes. You really know how to spoil a good mood! This Raffles can go to the devil! I'm not sleeping well since this guy appeared, and every night I'm uneasy about demons. It's like Raffles has already plundered my safe. Goddamn, I want no more of those night owls. But call in Miss Walton."

The accountant now left the room, while Brown went to the safe next to the desk and examined its dark exterior surface and bare bolts.

"I'm actually nervous," he murmured. He could not get over his fear that Raffles was already sitting inside his closed safe.

Again he snorted about various locksmiths, changed the combination and wrote it down. When he had finished Miss Walton entered.

She was a young woman wearing modest clothing, but had infinite charm in her narrow, delicate face.

Hesitantly she lingered in the doorway.

"Come closer, my dear child!" laughed Brown, and his little eyes lied. His awakening sensuality banished all thoughts of Raffles.

He stood over her, seized her with his meaty, ringed fingers and by her elegant slender hand led her to a Turkish chair.

This familiarity startled Miss Walton as if she had seen a spider. An inexplicable fear crept over her.

Brown snapped up the chair next to hers, and in turn touched her hand and stroked it, while tenderly looking into the young lady's eyes. His behavior brought shame burning red in Miss Walton's face.

"What beautiful hands you have!" Brown started the conversation; "fingers which are much too good for the coarse clerk duties which only needs them to gather up silk rods, but which should be adorned by diamonds!"

The young girl was too inexperienced to know her boss'

intentions, and although the great broker's touch gave her a painful feeling but she didn't dare wrest her hand from his.

She assumed the fifty-year-old man would have paternal benevolence toward her.

But holding his hand could be seen as a sign of consent.

A violent horror shot through the young woman.

Her female instincts made her realize suddenly the danger she was in, and what the scoundrel coveted.

She quickly stood up and said: "It's already late, Mr. Brown, I have a sick mother at home and she gets restless when I'm absent for too long, so please allow me to leave."

"Ah," replied her boss, "it's not that late. As for you mother, she should have the best of care, and all I ask is that you be nice to me."

Miss Walton looked at him with big, burning eyes, and a hot fear rose in her. She stood up hastily, and the wholesaler did the same and took her hand again.

His face was twisted by a brutal laugh, his eye lit up as he greedily took her arm; and as he pulled her back to him she protested: "Let me go. I have to leave!"

"Not so fast, my dear," Brown whispered in a hoarse, excited voice, "chat with me for an hour. You'll be home soon enough, and you should be grateful to me that you're still here."

He moved forward to embrace her, but she jumped aside and anxiously shouted: "Let me go or I'll call for help!"

"Oh," said the libertine, "you're a wild cat! Scream all

9

you want. There's no one to help you. We're alone in the office."

Miss Walton looked around anxiously for a means to escape. Brown, however, barred her way to the door.

Then she saw through the ground-floor window a tall, slender man was standing, just having bought an evening paper from a newsboy.

And the instant Mr. Brown tried to touch her again, she ran like lightning to the window and before the wholesaler could stop her she opened it and called out to the parties in front of the building.

"Please help me! This man is assaulting me!"

Amazed, her target turned around.

The young woman looked for a moment into a pair of large, dark eyes and saw a dark face tanned by the sun. The stranger bowed and replied:

"I'll be right there."

Miss Walton at the window returned a sigh of relief.

His face distorted with rage, Mr. Brown clenched his fists and shouted: "Fool! You'll pay for this!"

But at that moment also appeared in the room a stranger.

"What's going on here? Get out of my office before I call the police," yelled the merchant.

Without a word of acknowledgement, the stranger turned to Miss Walton and said: "How can I help you? I heard that you were being molested."

Miss Walton looked to her liberator for help and

answered: "Please take me out of this house. That man has insulted me in a shameless fashion."

The stranger understood the situation immediately; he saw the merchant with his contracted eyebrows fixed, walked up to him and dismissively said, "You're pathetic."

"Get out of my office," he gaspingly reprimanded in impotent rage.

The invader again looked at him scornfully and then turned to Miss Walton and said, "Please, come with me."

The young woman nodded thanks and left the room with him.

"You're fired!" cried the wholesaler after her.

The savior chuckled and brought Miss Walton to the door leading outside where she gave him more words of thanks. He addressed her again:

"It would help if you told me your address," he said.

Without hesitation, Miss Walton handed him a business card with her apartment number.

The stranger politely bowed and offered her his hand in farewell.

With gratitude the young woman wanted to bow down and kiss the stranger's hand. However, he hastily pulled it back.

"Go now, and thank God that he sent me to protect you," he said in soft, sonorous tones that fell upon the young woman's ear.

The thought of her sick mother drove her hurriedly

away. She did not see that the stranger, instead of following her, stepped back to the office door and reentered.

The intruder paused for several seconds, then reached into his pocket, pulled out a black mask, and turned to Mr. Brown's office.

The wholesaler was about to leave his private office, hat on his head. He had already apparently already forgotten about the unpleasant affair, softly whistling a tune from "The Merry Widow" and lit a cigar.

Suddenly, however, as he held up the match to light it, he suddenly paused.

A frosty feeling of fear ran down his back. Right in front of him, as if he grew out of the ground, a masked man pointed a revolver at him.

"You have company," a threatening voice echoed in Brown's ears. "I'm pleased to make your acquaintance, and hope this will be pleasant business."

The clerk was too scared to say another word and his knees trembled, the room began spinning and he went black.

"Follow me!" order the masked man in harsh tones, and Brown involuntarily obeyed. It was not possible for him to even consider resisting.

The way the two men went led to a space in a secluded corridor behind the office, and which served as the employee toilet. Here was a closet for their things.

The masked man opened it and ordered Brown to step

inside.

"Your wallet, my lord," were the next words the wholesaler heard, and trembling he obeyed in a way so satisfactory the robber continued:

"For your safe, today I don't have time. But don't worry, I'll come back for it." Then he locked the closet door and left the room.

Back in the office the masked man opened the wallet and took out several pound notes. Then he looked for some envelopes carrying the Brown company logo and divided up the bills.

At Brown's desk he wrote on each envelope:

"Put this to good use.
John Raffles."

He laughed softly and pressed on each envelope a seal, which was a skull and crossbones. Then he went to the employees' individual desks and left them there.

He looked at the items which remained in the stolen wallet. Only one thing interested him. It was a letter from the desk of an Oxford Street banker named James Gordon to Mr. Brown and read:

"My Dear Mr. Brown!
"Our last exchange was brilliantly profitable. Dr. Walter

has finally accepted our offer after I threatened to sue him. I have redeemed a £200 credit. Send me another patsy soon. The deal was worth it.

"Best Regards,

"James Gordon"

"This is a man I'd like to know," said Raffles, "such honorable gentlemen are my meat." He put the letter into his pocket, took off his mask and left the office.

After he exited he heard pounding on a door, caused by the locked-up broker.

Raffles laughed briefly, walked out to the road and disappeared.

Outside the newsboys still roared about his latest antics, not knowing he just performed a new one.

Chapter II

A Rogue Banker

In his small business office in London's Oxford Street sat banker James Gordon working on some large deposits he organized by rolling coins into wrappers and bills into bundles and putting them in a fine lock box.

He was a small, misshapen man with a pockmarked face that clearly bore an expression of cunning and greed.

The banker had just closed the safe when there was a knock on the door of his modest office.

With an unpleasant, hoarse voice he said, "Come in." An old woman of about 50 years old timidly stood in the doorway. With a sharp glance the businessman looked at her. "What do you want?" he curtly asked and sat down in the chair behind his desk.

"Forgive me," stammered the visitor, "my name is Mrs.

Annie Walton; I read in a newspaper ad that you lend money."

"But that is my business," said the banker. "Why do you need money?"

"Yes," the woman replied in a low voice. "I'm desperate. My husband died a year ago and my daughter needs help."

"Can you give me collateral?"

The banker drummed his boyish fingers on his desktop, because the old woman looked at him with a puzzled expression and did not answer his question.

"Well, are you going to answer or don't you understand?" he muttered gruffly after a prolonged silence. "I want to know whether you can give me any collateral?"

"Sir," replied the old woman, trembling and her eyes filling with tears, "I have only a few small belongs, which are only worth a pound sterling."

Banker Gordon let out a faint, whistling sneer and then said, laughing brutally, "Do you take me for a fool? Then every beggar across London, Whitechapel and East End will be trying to borrow money from me. Puh! You scoundrels have nothing yet want us to lend you money without collateral. Ha-ha!"

The woman looked at him anxiously. Her face clearly reflected the deepest despair about her situation.

"Sir," she said, "I am seriously ill and have dragged myself here to get help."

"Then you should have stayed at home and not wasted my time," Banker Gordon said roughly.

"Yes, but what should I do? I am at my wit's end. I swear to you on my honor, sir, that when I'm healthy again I'll work day and night to repay what I borrowed."

"I can't wait that long," said Banker Gordon dryly. "Everybody is dying of hunger. Know that! But you say you have a daughter? Then why not send her to go work the streets of Piccadilly, or if she's not pretty enough then let her work in Whitechapel. Earn your bread from the street."

The woman blanched at these words, as she feared those London locations, where half the criminal world came out at night.

"Never!" she cried. "Sir, if you had children you would not speak so. What a terrible thing to say."

Banker Gordon shrugged his shoulders contemptuously, then made a short, imperious hand gesture toward the door and said, shortly: "Go and leave me be. I can't take your whining any more. Listen, I have work to do."

With tired movements the woman staggered out the door.

At that moment a young, elegant man there took the unfortunate woman's arm and told her: "Don't go yet, Mrs. Walton. I fortunately overheard through the cracked door your conversation and I can help you."

Hesitantly the woman followed him and they reentered the back office, and the stranger shut the door.

Banker Gordon stood up and stared with an uncertain

expression at the doorway. He examined the stranger's elegant dress and determined that he belonged to the noble social class.

The stranger carelessly pulled off his pearl-gray gloves, took his monocle from his right eye and lit a cigarette. The cylinder, as if it wanted to make a point, did not reduce. The man might have been 30 years old, his sparking eyes fixed decisively on the Banker Gordon.

This made him nervous and uneasy; he didn't know quite what to make of the intruder.

After judging the brilliant luxuriousness which adorned the gentleman's hands, he figured he could offer him a fine loan.

When the stranger made no move to speak but with a mocking smile blew his cigarette smoke into his face, James Gordon finally asked, "How can I help you?"

"With quite a bit," answered the stranger. "I learned your address during a short visit to Mr. Brown last night. It's nice to meet you."

When the banker heard the name of his business partner, his face cleared. Hs bowed politely, and gestured him to sit down and said:

"To whom do I have the honor?"

Quietly and firmly the stranger bent over and after a short paused replied:

"My name will be familiar to you. My name is..." he paused again and his speech became slow and measured: "John C. Raffles."

As if he had been bitten by a snake Banker Gordon jumped up from his chair and fumbled irresolutely for a revolver hidden under some securities.

"You're Raffles?" he asked, stuttering with fear, "Raffles, from the...the...the..."

"That's right," he interrupted the trembling man, "the same. They call me Raffles, the Great Unknown, the Master Thief whose sport it is to seek out inhuman bastards and rob them, draining racketeers' blood to make them pay for their sins...

"...But first," he turned to the silent Mrs. Walton sitting there, "how much money did you need, my dear woman? Fifty pounds, what?"

"No, no!" she stuttered. "Five pounds would have helped me."

"I know your daughter, madam," Raffles said, "and as coincidence would have it I came to her aid. But let's leave that and talk about business."

He turned to Gordon. "Now, pay the woman five pounds!" The banker wanted to say something, but an unknown fear paralyzed him.

Spellbound by the resolute expression of the stranger's eyes, he opened his safe and took out a five-pound note.

Trembling, he laid it on the desk.

"Take it!" Raffles commanded the woman, "the banker gives it to you with a joyful heart. It is the most decent thing he has ever done, as he is loaning you the money without interest, since he is a charitable man. You don't have to pay it back until you can make a good living again. He knows you're not in the best of health. In general, he is a very excellent human being, this Banker Gordon.

"Now go and leave me alone with him."

Thanking him warmly the unfortunate woman left the room. No sooner had the door closed behind her Raffles struck a different tone and said:

"I'm really pleased finally to get to meet London's most common racketeer and usurer. Now, I beg you," he said as he pulled a revolver from his elegant fur, "stay as calm as if you were in church."

With altering steps the banker knelt as commanded. He was completely paralyzed. Without protest he watched as John Raffles opened the safe and removed some large packages belonging to the besieged usurer, and put them in a small, yellow handbag.

An inarticulate sound, like that from a hobbled animal, came from the banker.

Raffles looked at him and smiled mockingly. "Did you say something? You're probably regretting that I finally have this load of notes to liberate, collected here from usurious exchanges and promissory notes from unfortunate victims. You'll be grateful to me, my dear sir, that I'm doing this for decent people; besides, if you want to stop me, you can call the

20

police. Since..." he laughed out loud again, lit a cigarette, closed his bag and continued: "I believe that they would get nothing but insight into the usury business, and that would be a splendid joke if it happened, since in addition to the harm you're getting from my visit, your freedom would suffer. That wouldn't be good for you, but would be great for mankind, freed from such a hideous insect after such a long time. I think that you are too cowardly to protest or come at me. Well, you can try but I'll enjoy turning you over to the police."

In the banker's ashen face came forward new features of hate and fear.

"You won't notify the police," he whispered in a hoarse voice, "how would that benefit you?"

"I told you," said John Raffles, "it benefits the general public to be free of you."

No sooner had these words fallen then the banker rose from his knees, raised his hand imploringly and whimpered for mercy.

But the master thief remained cold.

With an expression of disgust he looked at the pleading man and contemptuously said, "You are a coward, like all villains. But I'm just as ruthless as you have been when you mercilessly took advantage of the unfortunate."

Then Raffles took one of the usurer's business ledgers, seized its heavy strap with two hands, hit him powerfully on the head and laughed. "Something to remember me by."

The battering dropped Banker Gordon to the ground, stunned. Raffles watched him for a few seconds, then he drew from his pocket a small vial dripping liquid and pressed it to the face of the banker laying on the carpet before the fireplace.

Quietly he said to himself: "He must remain like this until the police arrive. Otherwise my fun will be spoiled."

Then the master thief took the bag containing the business vouchers and left the bank office.

He carefully locked the office door and gave it to an elevator boy and told him:

"Mr. Gordon has gone for two hours, and he instructed me to give you the key."

"All right!" replied the young man who took innocently.

Then John Raffles left the building.

Chapter III

The Terror of Scotland Yard

Police Captain Baxter of the London Special Branch was in his office, which handled Scotland Yard's pursuit of all of England's most notorious criminals. He stood with rapt attention before the telegraph receiver next to his desk and the secret reports which Morse's machine sent in sharp ticks to the secret commissioner from various forensic departments.

Nervously the inspector let the narrow strip of telegram slip through his fingers. Suddenly his eyes flared. As if he had seen a ghost he stared at the incoming telegram. His face was pale, he let out a loud, inarticulate squeal and then jumped to his desk. He hastily pressed a button on his intercom and after a few seconds several of his detectives rushed into his office.

"What is it, captain?" called Sergeant Tyler, a large, burly detective, to his superior.

"Spooks! A devilish piece of foolery," cried the obsessed inspector. "Take a look at this mysterious Boston telegram apparently sent by master thief John Raffles himself. He managed to establish a connection to our secret system. He must be working with the devil. We can't get any more confidential cables. He's able to intercept our most intimate messages. Goddamn, gentleman, this is Raffles's most amazing prank yet. See for yourself."

Curious, the officers thronged to Captain Baxter and started at the strips of telegraph paper, which read:

"POLICE CAPTAIN BAXTER SCOTLAND YARD EXCUSE ME FOR COMMUNICATING THIS WAY STOP THIS IS AN EARLY WARNING THAT WITHIN THE NEXT 24 HOURS I AM COMING TO ROB THE SAFE OF LORD LISTER STOP IN THE FUTURE I WILL USE THIS METHOD TO WARN YOU ABOUT MY NEXT WONDERFUL BUSINESS TRANSACTIONS STOP WITH THE HIGHEST ESTEEM FOR YOU AND SCOTLAND YARD RAFFLES."

"Raffles!" repeated the staff.

"Yes, gentlemen," said Baxter. "This John Raffles is driving me mad. I'm already obsessed with him. All the newspapers in England and abroad are amusing themselves free at our expense. It's too much! From now own, he's going to warn us about his intended crimes ahead of time.

"He wants to make you more comfortable, captain. He's certainly a polite human being," said Detective Marholm, whom London thugs called "the Bug" due to his physique. He smiled broadly, which made his boss angrier.

Captain Baxter slammed his fist on the desk and red-faced screamed with rage. "I'm glad you're having good time, Detective Marholm!"

"I can't deny," he replied, "that I'm really enjoying it; the man is impressive."

"He doesn't have to impress you. I'm going to jump into the deepest part of the Thames if I don't catch him this time."

"Has Sherlock Holmes responded to you?" Sgt. Tyler asked his boss.

The English policeman's face broke into an indignant expression at the mention of his famous colleague.

"The devil take me! Here's a letter from Mr. Holmes about this affair, and he writes that he's taking such legitimate pleasure in these criminal tricks that he didn't want to interfere and has declined Scotland Yard's request for help."

"That is," said Sergeant Tyler, "what Sherlock Holmes enjoys about Scotland Yard and he wants to show us that perhaps we can catch flies without him, but not criminals."

"The newspapers have the same opinion about us," said Detective Marholm. "Sherlock Holmes has been showing us up."

"This brings John Raffles back to mind," groaned

Captain Baxter. "London is quite amused. Goddamn, it's like he's the city's only criminal!"

At that moment the telephone rang. Tyler took the receiver while the rest waited in deep silence.

Suddenly the big burly man began to tremble, the color left his face and he had to support himself with his right hand on the desk. His colleagues stared at him.

"What happened, Tyler?" said Baxter.

The sergeant waved his hand for silence, then made a short, excited, almost strangled sound. "Yes," he said into the telephone, then hung up the receiver and said in a quick, official voice:

"We have to get to the bank office of James Gordon in Oxford Street. The banker is unconscious in front of his fireplace and missing from his safe is £3,865 sterling."

"Who called in the message?" said Capt. Baxter, preparing to leave.

"Who?" repeated Sergeant Tyler as he drew a breath. "The criminal himself!"

"Goddamn!" blurted out all the officers in unison.

"And to Captain Baxter," Tyler continued, "the burglar conveyed his best wishes and gave me his name all at once: John Raffles!"

It was like a bomb dropped. Several seconds passed in breathless silence, and then Baxter said:

"Let's move, people. Every second counts! The man will

drive me out of my mind!"

A few minutes later an automobile flew at top speed out of Scotland Yards's gate. It contained Inspector Baxter and four of the Yard's most experienced officers. Their destination was James Gordon's bank offices in Oxford Street.

In less than a quarter of an hour they stopped in front of a large office building. Hundreds of small businessmen had their quarters in the six-story edifice.

In the elevator the concierge brought the officers to the fourth floor to the permanent bank offices of James Gordon.

The door was locked.

Baxter removed a business card which was stuck into the door jam and read:

"The key to the office is with the elevator boy Tim."

He was in charge of the fourth elevator.

The boy was immediately summoned. He removed several keys from his trouser pocket and said that a gentleman gave it to him so Gordon could enter when he returned. He received a shilling for his trouble.

"What did the man look like?" asked Capt. Baxter.

"He was big, captain," answered the elevator boy, "he wore a thick black beard, a brown suit and hat and stuttered."

"Ah, we finally get closer to the Unknown," said Captain Baxter. "What color were his eyes?"

"I don't know. The gentleman wore dark, tinted glasses."

Detective Marholm laughed out loud.

27

"Let's not waste time," urged Sergeant Tyler and prompted Inspector Baxter to unlock the door.

They immediately entered the business office.

Everything was as it had been described by telephone. Before a small fireplace was the 70-year-old banker, and his eyes were closed. A sweet odor of knock-out drops, the dangerous narcotic used by London's underground, filled the room.

The policemen's efforts managed to awaken the unconscious man.

He soon recovered enough that he could answer the officers' questions, and his face twisted into an indignant expression.

"What's happening, gentlemen?"

The question was so unexpected that it completely baffled the detectives staring at the banker.

"You have been robbed," said Captain. Baxter, pointing at the open safe.

The banker made an indifferent hand gesture and asked, "Who are you?"

Baxter and his detectives believed that the banker was still suffering from the anesthetic's effects, and Detective Marholm said to the chief:

"Give the banker a few minutes until he can recover; you can see for yourself he doesn't even remember what happened."

Gordon's bird-like, pointed nose, reminiscent of a hawk, flushed red with anger. With his unpleasant, hoarse voice he yelled at the detectives:

"I'll ask again. Why are you in my office? What do you intend to do with me?"

Chief Inspector Baxter threw it back like a rock, making his golden badge visible on his breast and said: "We are officers of the SB and have been notified that you have been robbed."

"Who told you that?"

"The thief himself," said Baxter.

"You're crazy," screamed Gordon. "You're crazy. I know better than you do."

The detectives did not know what to make of the banker's strange behavior.

"You want to trick us?" cried Captain Baxter angrily.

The banker's small, deformed shape faced them and with a commanding gesture pointed to the door and grunted:

"If you don't leave my office immediately I'll call the next police station to help. There's nothing here for you to see. I don't need you. Get out!"

Completely stunned the amazed detectives withdrew since they had to respect his rights under English law, and moved to the door.

Captain Baxter then turned back to the angry banker and said, "Think about what you're doing, mister. You've been attacked and robbed, and had £3,865 sterling stolen from you."

"Take care of your own business and not mine," roared the banker, cherry red with anger. "I repeat, I did not call you...and now for the last time, get out of my office!"

With this prompt the officers had no choice but to leave.

Outside in the corridor they stood and looked at each other as if they were all insane. A venomous and loud laugh came from Gordon and filled the space.

"That was the strangest thing I have ever seen," he said to Detective Sergeant Tyler after a pause. "But the devil hang me if I can understand it.

"The rogue told us everything about how he robbed the man and it was just as he said, before we were shown the door."

At that moment a messenger boy hurried in and cried aloud Inspector Baxter's name.

"Here!" he said, "here I am!"

The messenger gave him an envelope on which in large letters was printed the name Captain Baxter, and Banker Gordon's Oxford Street address.

He hastily tore open the envelope and a ten-pound note and a written message were inside.

The chief's eyes almost jumped out of his head as he read:

"For your efforts on the occasion of your slump I'm sending £10 and I hope that you all use it to buy yourself a nice breakfast.

"Raffles."

In impotent fury Baxter crumpled up the envelope. He was too embarrassed to tell his officers what it said.

"We'll go see Lord Lister," he told the detectives, "and when Scotland Yard becomes mobile he won't be able to rob the lord when we catch him. The men must not believe he's in league with the devil."

Baxter did not see the Bug's smiling face.

Detective Malcolm was amused more than he had ever been in his career.

Chapter IV

An Unfortunate Friend

The same evening a colorful, ragtag group of diverse people of gathered in the lobby of the small, mansion-like house of Lord Lister in Regent Park.

All carried telegrams and in quiet tones talked about the strange content of the dispatches which all contained identical text:

"Come to me at once for final settlement of your business with Banker Gordon. Lord Lister. Regent Park 2."

The door opened.

In the lobby from an interior sitting room came a young, slender person of about 30: Lord Edward Lister. A somewhat younger secretary carrying a thick leather wallet followed him.

The gathered people considered questioning the young lord, especially the women who among them felt the most attraction toward him.

He had an even, excellent build and a fresh face which betrayed both pride and honor. His big black eyes looked at the group and the peer said in a sonorous voice:

"I received this afternoon from Banker Gordon this wallet, and he asked me to dismiss the liabilities he has against you."

"Goddamn that dangerous London cutthroat and usurer!" cried a woman, and another said aloud:

"The curse is lifted; this will be a big relief to my family who're in this leech's hands; like me, it happens to all those he touches."

As one they cheered.

Lord Lister watched them.

In most of their faces was deep hate, grief, misery and worry.

"I know why you call this man a cutthroat. Unfortunately the law is unable to punish such people. Even worse than criminals are these smoothly refined rogues that break to the rules behind the scenes, and enjoy the law's protection. Therefore I say you have claim against Banker Gordon, and I free you from your liabilities.

"Here, my friends, I return to you all the promissory notes and debts to which you signed away your hearts and souls to this great London scoundrel.

"God protect you, and in the future may you never again

fall into such a rogue's hands.

"Open the wallet, Charlie!"

The unfortunate people felt as if they were in a dream. It was impossible. It was like a miracle from heaven.

Timidly and suspiciously they took the cursed documents, and looked down on them as evil and snorted, as though they doubted their authenticity.

But it was not possible they were forged.

They all held in their hands the promissory notes and I.O.U.s that had once belonged to the bloodsucker.

They felt infinite gratitude to their strange benefactor Lord Lister.

Above all, with teary eyes they wanted to shake his hand, but when they looked for him he was gone.

Only the secretary remained, and he exhorted them to go home.

Slowly the lobby emptied, and soon evening drew on the small villa.

##

In his study before the fireplace Lord Lister sat in a comfortable lounge chair and smoked his ubiquitous cigarette.

His clean-cut face, which usually showed a serious, melancholy expression, looked thoughtfully into the dancing flames.

Close by sat his private secretary and friend Charlie Brand.

The study was furnished with simple but noble elegance.

Nearby was a wide sliding door leading to the bedroom. Beside it was an old Flemish grandfather clock, and the door's right side was a safe.

A servant entered and with a deep bow handed Lord Lister the newest headlines:

"Raffles at work!"

"Scotland Yard duped!"

"The Master Thief's latest trick!"

"A London banker who denies he was robbed!"

Lord Lister laughed quietly and after reading each sensational headline and article passed the newspapers across to his friend.

While Charlie Brand studied them the noble man watched with intense interest his friend's face; and saw it turn pale.

The peer lit a new cigarette. When he was finished, Charlie Brand said, "Edward, are you connected to Banker Gordon?"

Lord Lister laughed again quietly, flicked his cigarette ash into the chimney fire, shrugged indifferently and answered:

"Me? Connected? Why do you think so?"

"Yes, have you read, Edward, that the man was robbed this morning?"

"So the police believe. The men of Scotland Yard. The so-called victim asserts the contrary," he replied.

"It's the weirdest thing I've ever read," said Charlie Brand.

"No way, replied Lord Lister; "if I were Sherlock Holmes I would quickly untie this knot."

"And how?"

Charlie Brand looked with rapt attention at his friend.

"Very simple. The victim has not come forward and would rather hide his loss since a police investigation would send him to jail."

"You would have made an excellent detective!"

"Indeed," said the lord. "A year ago I began to find this life to be extremely boring. I wondered if I could be in Sherlock Holmes' company, and hunt down criminals.

"After carefully considering the matter I came to the conclusion that if one want to use crime as sport, it would mean that it would be more interesting to be the prey than the hunter, or better put to be the criminal instead of the detective. Understand me, Charlie, I'm only speaking of this thing as a matter of sport.

"Look, Charlie, such a criminal needs twice as much energy, guile and other qualities than the detective. It's quite a challenge."

"Hearing you speak, one might believe that you have a strong affinity for this Unknown Raffles."

"Oh, yes. This Raffles is a thief within the meaning of racketeers, but he fights practically against rogue social and financial imposters protected by the law. And this mystery man shows us he can do more with the stolen goods than most of London's so-called Christian charities. In the most infamous neighborhoods of the city, in the most wretched hollows of poverty, in the suburbs the name of Raffles is sacrosanct. Just today at noon he offered me the undoubtedly stolen exchanges and promissory notes belonging to Banker Gordon which I did not stop from being returned to their rightful owners."

"A remarkable man," said Charlie thoughtfully. "The whole world speaks of him and the inhabitants of the west side tremble when they hear his name."

"Yes," said Lister. "The rich may tremble and the poor rejoice!"

At this moment entered the old valet Fred.

He handed him a business card on a silver platter.

A joyous red color filled the lord's face as he read the name, and then said:

"Send the lady in to me. And you, Charlie," he turned to his friend, "you should leave now. Tonight I am prevented from occupying myself with historical studies."

Charlie Brand rose, took his employer's hand and said goodbye.

As soon as he walked out of the room a young lady wearing a long veil entered.

"Miss Walton, my dear friend," said the lord who got up and offered to the woman his outstretched hand.

Gallantly he bowed and kissed her right hand and said:

"I took the liberty of writing to you. I had to see you again. I was extremely pleased that you have come."

"I owe you a great deal of thanks, my Lord," she said simply.

Then she pulled back the veil to reveal a nice gift, a Madonna-like countenance from which two large blue child's eyes gazed at the peer. They contrasted sharply with her profoundly black hair.

Lord Lister led her to the chair by the fireplace and turned to face her.

"I need your help," he said, and her beautiful eyes filled with tears.

"My mother is seriously ill, and everything our father left us has been sold. I tried everywhere to find work, but you know what happened to me in my last position. Oh, it's horrible. It's like they're all Mr. Brown everywhere. As soon as I have a position for a few days they make me all sorts of promises and then try to seduce me and when I resist I'm out of a job again."

"Poor child," whispered Lord Lister. "I know what happens and how unfortunate girls are forced to walk the streets. If I had a rod I would flog every one of those wretches that drive women to such desperate measures. But now, let me tell you how you can help me."

She looked at him with her beautiful eyes, and after a few thanks for answering her and helping her mother with the money she continued.

"It is very difficult for a man who has never had to do it, to ask for help. But I know I'll never be a submissive working woman."

"Yes, you're right," said Lord Lister, "unscrupulous businessmen believe that money gives them the right to do anything, to buy anything, to live as he likes and requires that workers honor him and be treated like slaves. But let's drop this unpleasant topic. I wrote to you because I'm leaving tomorrow for a few months, my dear woman, and I have a large amount of copying to be done. It would please me if you could work for me for a few months. You can do this work at home while you are looking after your sick mother."

He went to a cabinet and took out five large volumes of world history.

"I can't ask my servants, which you have seen, to do this, because as I have said I am going away for an indefinite time. Take this money as an advance."

He reached into his breast pocket and pulled out a portfolio, took an envelope from his desk and put some money into it.

He closed it and with a chivalrous bow handed it to the young woman.

She bent over to try to kiss his hand again. But he quickly pulled it back and said:

"No, my dear girl, that does not befit me. Now go home

39

and see about your mother. And if it appears that I have overpaid you, I'm used to paying princely sums. I ask you to use the money without any more gratitude."

The valet came in and announced: "Police Captain Baxter of Scotland Yard."

"Baxter?" said Miss Walton as fear spread across her face.

Lord Lister looked surprised.

"What is it, Miss Walton?"

Trembling she answered.

"Allow me to leave the house without seeing this man. He is a relative of mine, a hard-hearted, selfish man who responded to my pleadings about my mother by showing me the door. He said rabble like us do not deserve anything but should jump into the Thames. And that the world would not miss us."

"A neat saint," replied Lister. When he looked at Miss Walton's eyes he noticed that they filled with tears. With a soft, kindly smile he joined her and held her hand. An infinitely soothing feeling rippled through the young woman. Lister no longer seemed like a stranger, but like a brother.

"How can I thank you?" she whispered as her eyes met his.

He felt her arousal and all her involuntary desires.

In an instant he experienced hot longing for this beautiful woman, pulled her to his breast and kissed her chaste, red lips.

If anyone had the right to do so, it was him. Without him

she would dishonored, or perhaps had thrown herself into the Thames.

They looked at each other deeply for several seconds and in that time the two people were wrapped tightly by a love thread.

Lord Lister regained his control. He bent down and silently kissed the girl's forehead. Then he asked her to call him by his first name. "Go on home, Miss Helen, God bless you. I may need your help again."

As he turned the doorknob he called the valet and asked her to escort Miss Walton home. They left by a back entrance.

As the door closed behind them, his eyes with a wistful expression stared after her, and he quietly said to himself: "It's too late for me, given the path which I have chosen. There's no room for love to awaken. If I had met her four months ago everything would have been different."

His face was serious again. He sat down in the lounge chair in front of the fireplace, smoking a new cigarette. After a few minutes he donned a monocle and assumed the lax attitude the incoming Police Captain Baxter would expect.

Chapter V

The Slump

"I come to your rescue," reported Police Captain Baxter, as he faced Lord Lister. A mocking smile played around the gentleman's mouth, and he replied quizzically:

"To my rescue? This is extremely interesting to me. I didn't know I needed rescuing. Or am I missing something?"

He craned his amazingly athletic body, which towered at least a head over the police inspector.

"It's not an attack on your person," he said.

"I would like to know more about this inhuman threat!" laughed the Lord. "I have received several boxing awards and am also in my club known as one of the best fencers and pistol shootists. I can hit a half a penny between a thumb and forefinger."

"As I said," repeated Baxter, "it's not an attack on your

person, but an attack to steal your property."

But Lister indicated his safe and quietly said,

"My property is secure in there, and it would take considerable difficulty to get at it. One could grow old trying."

"Nevertheless, one of London's most dangerous burglars will pay you a visit today to try to seize your valuables."

Lord Lister laughed and cried, "What fun. How do you know the burglar is planning to steal from me?"

The officer thumped himself in the chest and spoke in a loud and supercilious tone:

"Scotland Yard knows everything! We are called the world's most famous secret police!"

"No doubt," Lord Lister laughed teasingly.

Baxter noticed this, and a little nervously continued.

"Does your Lordship seem to have a somewhat lower judgment of our profession because of our last failed strike against the unknown Raffles?"

"Well," he answered and lit a new cigarette, "you can't say that you've got Raffles cornered."

"I'll get him, but we have to understand how to deal with this genie and oddly enough we get no support from the public in our struggle against him. Undoubtedly this situation has also helped keep the rogue innocuous."

Lord Lister smoked thoughtfully and considered the idea for a bit.

"You can't argue with certainty. But to get to our thing,

so the burglar is supposed to visit me tonight. If he does he'll find a good haul since yesterday I acquired £20,000 sterling and the money has not been put yet in my bank. I also already considered the possibility of theft, and for this reason have shared with you the total amount. One half is there housed in my safe, the rest is in an iron box in my bedroom by the bed. See it there." He pointed through the open door and to a metal box, which stood on a rug next to the bed.

"Very practical," said Baxter, "but the thief could rob the safe."

"Well, fair enough," the lord said carelessly. "He should try that feat, since I'm insured against loss due to burglary and theft. I'm not worried about it. The insurance company will reimburse me for any damage or loss."

After a short pause the police officer finally said: "It's up to me and Scotland Yard to seize the intruder, and I would like to ask you to allow me and my officers to monitor your home tonight."

"Very well," nodded the lord. "My apartment is at your disposal. Please excuse me, however. It's already a quarter to eight, and I have to meet a friend. My valet," he rang for him, "will provide everything that you may require. By the way, Mr. Baxter, what sort of burglar is it that wants to honor me?"

"Yes, it's the famous Raffles," was the reply,

"Raffles? Gee, that's an interesting guy I'd like to meet. I'll tell my friend that I'm indisposed and will keep you

44

company. Maybe together we can finally successfully capture this innocuous burglar."

"Most Certainly," affirmed Baxter.

"So, when he comes," interposed the Lord, "but," he continued, "I will immediately rush my car to the theater and personally tell my friend that I'm not free this evening, and will be back by 10 o'clock."

"And I will notify my officers," were the captain's final words.

He looked as Lord Lister, who left with a quick "Goodbye" and went into his bedroom and took a fur from an armchair.

Then the police captain left the room. In the entrance hall waited his officers. They were the same ones that visited Banker Gordon.

They discussed how to proceed and struck on a course of action. He would spend the night in Lord Lister's study. Two officers would be posted in the lobby, and one in the upper chambers.

This way the villa was so well-guarded it was like a mouse trying to escape a cat. No entrance or exit was unobserved.

The captain called for the valet and proceeded to the study.

Lord Lister appeared to have already left, since the electric lights were turned off in both the study and bedroom and they were dark.

An officer turned the light back on and showed Baxter the location of the switch. It was close to the fireplace.

They both examined the bedroom. A wide door that could slide into the wall on either side separated the bedroom and study.

In the former was only a small window protected by an iron railing. From here on the left was a small bathroom. There was no other entrance to the bedroom or bathroom, the only access being the study.

The police officer looked over all the room again closely, picked up the blankets, opened the closet and even took out all the clothes to make sure no one was hiding inside.

The activity and caution amused the valet, who felt himself moved to say: "You really should not overlook even the smallest speck of dust in your investigation."

"I should think so," replied Baxter, thumping his chest, "we won't overlook anything, not even a bug."

"Do you have any other requests?" said the servant.

"No, you go relax," he responded, and the valet left the study. The captain sat in the chair before the fire and began to read the evening paper. After an hour he put the newspaper aside and pulled from his pocket an electric safety lamp, and after confirming it worked properly placed it on the fireplace.

Then he examined his Browning pistol and put the gun in his jacket pocket so it would be handy if needed.

Nothing broke the house's silence. Everything was quiet. Not a sound betrayed the detective's presence.

Deep in the study's darkness Captain Baxter was able to discern an object. The swinging of the great clock's massive pendulum was the only sound he heard. The clock stood against the wall, behind which was the bedroom and bathroom.

The loud bell now hit the tenth hour.

But, what was that? Baxter listened with bated breath. When the clock's strikes subsided he heard from the bedroom a small noise, like a chisel on steel.

Lynx-like the detective's eyes bored into the darkness, and he could recognize the dim outline of a form next to the bed.

For a moment he hesitated, his pulse quickening.

He believed it was an illusion, since it seemed impossible that anyone could have slipped into the bedroom, and he had searched everything and everywhere and nobody could have been hiding there.

Then he heard a sharp sound, a cracking as when a metal container is violently broken open.

In an instant the police captain had torn his Browning from his pocket and turned on the electric lamp. His eyes eventually focused on the clandestine figure. Finally caught! went him through his mind. He saw in the bedroom next to the iron box a man in an elegant dress suit, top hat on his head and a black mask over his face.

"Stop!" cried Baxter in a commanding tone, "or I'll

47

shoot!"

But the masked man also raised his revolver, so that Baxter was forced to turn off the light, so darkness could protect him from bullets.

At the same moment he fired. He had to, because at once something unexpected happened: The masked man jumped to the sliding door and closed it before the captain was able to stop him.

Now his officers rushed into the room, alarmed by the shot.

Baxter switched on the light again, and cried:

"We have him! Finally I have the infamous Raffles. In there he sits, like a mouse in a trap that he cannot escape. Watch Out! Take out your revolvers, people. Forward!"

He jumped to the sliding door, perspiring, and pushed it open.

A moment later the invaders faltered. The room was completely dark and there was nothing to see besides the broken steel box.

They breathlessly tore apart the bed and opened the closet. They found no one.

"He's in the bathroom," said Detective Marholm and tried to open the door.

It didn't budge and remained closed.

Together the officers tried to force it open. It apparently was held by an iron bar inside.

The obstruction proved to be very strong, because all four men had to push against it.

While the policemen wasted their time, suddenly the door of the study's large Flemish grandfather clock opened, and from it stepped a masked man.

The piece of furniture set against the wall was adjacent to the bedroom and bathroom and had a secret door built into it.

The timepiece was connected via a passage to the bathroom, hidden behind a sliding door.

None of the searchers suspected that the apparently solid wood wall led to the study.

For a moment the masked man peeked around the corner to the officers, and then quick as a tiger he closed the sliding door, threw it with a lightning fast jerk and slid a bolt.

He was completely hidden in there from the officers.

With cool deliberation the masked man now hastened to the safe and opened it with a secret key he removed from his pocket, took out a packet and in a moment was gone from the room.

At the same time officers rattled the closed door and after some desperate minutes broke it down.

Despite their excitement they stood still for a moment as if turned to stone.

The door of the safe was wide open, and the inside they saw was dark and empty.

"Devil!" Baxter gritted his teeth, "Sorcery! Magic! The

safe is empty!"

"Indeed," said Detective Marholm "That's self-evident."

"Come on! We must find him," ordered the captain and they hurried to the door of the room.

He rushed after the detectives.

But when he opened the portal in bounced Lord Lister and his friend Charlie Brand together.

"Hello!" cried the peer, "Good evening, gentlemen! Why are you in such a hurry, Mr. Baxter?"

"Have you seen Raffles?" he cried.

"Me? No," laughed Lord Lister. "I've come from of the club just to help you catch him, but maybe you saw him?"

"Sirrrr," the inspector went on, "My Lord, you're making fun of me. But joking aside, I actually did see him. Here in your bedroom that he robbed and your office."

"Well, what more" asked the lord calmly. "Did you let him get away?"

Inspector Baxter did not answer. Instead, the Bug said:

"Yes, my Lord! We were so polite as to let him escape with the help of the Lord Police Inspector"

"Shut up!" Baxter shouted angrily. "The man has made a pact with the devil! He got away. See, my Lord, he escaped from that room, despite strict surveillance, despite my best officers. I even kept the entrance under watch and there's no other way into this room, as your lordship knows. When I found him we rushed out and threw the sliding door closed. When we opened the door he locked himself in the bathroom and bolted the door."

"A strange man!" laughed Lord Lister. "Was he in there taking a bath?"

"He was not, your Lordship," said Detective Marholm, "but he apparently traveled through the water pipes while we looked at the empty room, and with all coziness opened your safe and stole everything inside it.

"So you see, Inspector Baxter," he turned to his boss, "Raffles again has kept his word."

"He's driving me mad!" groaned the captain.

Lord Lister with a mocking smile looked at the safe when his secretary entered. With a few words he explained the situation, then opened his wallet and removed an insurance policy against theft and loss and handed it to his friend and confidant.

"Tomorrow morning," he said, "take this document to the insurance company and request the amount that has been stolen from me by the brilliant Raffles, despite police protection. And now, gentlemen detectives, I will give you some good advice. If Raffles notifies you again that he intends to visit me, don't bother yourselves about it and kindly let me alone. You don't need to be here for him to steal from me, I can do that myself."

The embarrassed Police Inspector Baxter and his officers left the house at once.

After the door was closed and locked behind them, Lord

Lister laughed out loud and said to his friend Charlie:

"Tomorrow we travel to Berlin; I want to visit an old friend of mine there."

"Yes, but in more detail," he replied, "I do not understand the whole thing. Did you actually have £20,000 sterling in the safe?"

"No!" his good friend quietly said. "Just a few packages of unpaid bills."

"Hmm," said Charlie Brand, and his face had a wistful expression, as if he did not quite understand what his friend was saying, "That's not clear to me all."

"Well, my boy," said the latter, "do you not understand that the unpaid bills that the police let a certain Unknown Raffles steal from me will be reimbursed by the insurance company for £20,000 sterling? It was just as well I not have anything more in the safe. The main thing is that I have the testimony from Police Inspector Baxter and his detectives that amount was indeed stolen and the insurance company needs to pay for it. Well, there you are! It's just business."

"Damn!" Charlie marveled, "that's a splendid idea. But, my dear friend, where did Raffles come from?"

Lord Lister took out a cigarette and lit it. Then he blew very slowly and leisurely turned big smoke rings into the air and said with a fine smile on his face:

"Yes, my dear boy, you do not need to know; it is sufficient to me that you are my good and faithful Charlie, who thank God doesn't have to understand everything. As for Raffles, my boy, Raffles, he's my idol."

Chapter VI

Conspirators

Shortly after the police left Banker James Gordon, he finished his business in his bank office and went down to Oxford Street in the direction of the Tower of London.

At the Thames he boarded an electric train which brought him to the Tower Bridge.

Here by the Tower, located at England's proud Royal Castle, there is a neighborhood whose residents are the most feared and dangerous criminals in London.

A myriad of little streets in this ancient area, having houses with deep basements, provided a wonderful haven for the light-shunning rabble of the English capital.

In one of these streets lived Mr. Govern, an Irish moneylender, whom the police nicknamed "The Black Jack".

The Holy Brotherhood held him as one of the cleverest

and most refined fences in the metropolis.

Nevertheless, he obviously did business of all kinds with pickpockets, professional criminals, whores and pimps, but never succeeded in moving up to a higher level of criminality.

The Black Jack was a simple smuggler.

There were rumors that he owned several houses and was an investor in a big company.

The store which he occupied was filled with bales of goods of all kinds: Barrels with hardtack, sides of American bacon, silk dresses, gold bars, ambergris-scented suits, furniture and boxes which filled the small, cramped room so tightly that only a narrow passage right through the showroom to the greasy counter remained, behind which the Black Jack served his customers from morning till night.

An old maritime lamp burned, or it would have been pitch-dark.

Banker Gordon and Black Jack welcomed each other like old friends. The men of honor: spent many years together in such greasy and dirty shops.

By means of a secret spring behind his counter the pawnbroker locked the front door. He always did this when his friend James Gordon made a business trip to his office.

Having thus insured they would not be interrupted, he offered the banker a cigar, which he recommended by saying:

"An excellent brand, they arrived fresh in the harbor from Havana yesterday. Half-Ear stole them from the boat shed.

Unfortunately, he only got fifty pieces, as they were well-guarded, since they are intended for the royal household."

But James Gordon did not seem to be able to enjoy it despite its excellent quality and taste.

After he smoked some it, he turned to the Black Jack and told him the story of the incident with the brilliant Raffles.

Anger and hatred flashed in the usurer's eyes, and he clenched his fists as he cried:

"I must get my property back. This dog Raffles will know who he's dealing with. Two inches of cold iron between his ribs will be the price for the trick he played on me."

His business friend scratched his nappy hair and finally said after prolonged contemplation:

"Goddam, my boy, from our business I've always had the greatest confidence in you, and I don't care that sometimes my friends may have make someone take the journey to the afterlife, but in this case—I don't quite know, James, if you've studied this opponent that outsmarted you. Who is he?"

The banker leaned very close to his confidant's ear and whispered:

"Lord Lister!"

His sidekick jumped in astonishment at the mention of the reputable name and looked the banker, as if he did not quite understand him, and finally after a longer pause, asked:

"How do you know?"

Gordon took out a letter and gave it to Black Jack, who

read this inscription: "Mr. Lyon, Booth II, London. By special delivery."

"This is your cover address, your secret office," said the pawnbroker.

"So it is," rejoined the banker. "Chance led me there before I went to you, and this letter had come in. Read it."

Jack pulled the letter out and scanned the contents:

"Dear Sir!

"I have to return to you your bank deposits and interest notes. Please visit me tonight.

"Lord Edward Lister, Regent Park."

For a second time he studied the letter.

"I understand what happened last night!" he said at last.

"But," cried James Gordon, "listen to me: Raffles took all my bills and investment securities, as well as my main book listing the accounts of my clients. From this he took the addresses and wrote to them to give back the stolen items. As you know I have a secret account at the Bank of England under the name of Lyon, and Raffles, believing that this was also one of my clients, wrote the letter, signed "Lord Edward Lister": thus legally the lord and Raffles are one and the same person."

"The devil!" roared the pawnbroker, "that would be the most amazing operation I ever experienced."

"Who do you have on hand?" Gordon asked without paying attention to his comrade's excitement. "I need at once two of your best safecrackers so we can plan to visit the dog tonight and try to retrieve my property before he gives away it to my customers."

"I don't understand him!" Jack muttered, still staring at the letter. "The man must be a fool, yet still this thief takes no other pleasure than stealing. This Raffles could teach old Hob a few things! Well, no matter, I'll call up two of my best people right away."

He unplugged a pipe that led into the ground, said a few words into it and listened intently.

After some time could be heard as if from a distance three muffled words.

"They're there and will come right away!" Jack referred to his trusted friends on the other side of the strange phone.

After a few minutes came from an old cabinet that stood in the store a faint throbbing.

The junk dealer at once stood up, and through the ancient door of the closet came two dangerous and suspicious-looking subjects who crawled through the hanging clothes to stand at the counter in front of the usurers.

Then Jack tightly closed the closet door and explained to the banker: "This is my secret exit to the basement and it has saved from the gallows many of the persecuted for whom nobody would give a penny and who are dogged by Scotland Yard.

"Well, boys, I have a job for you."

"All right!" replied the larger of the two men, whose face

was disfigured by a horrible scar, after a knife cut through the middle of his cheek and had removed half his nose.

His former comrades did this to him because he had betrayed one of them to Scotland Yard, and the underworld now called him "the Pig". His confederate was a serious criminal known as "Half-Ear".

"So what's the job, boy?" he asked Govern.

He puffed his fine cigar and replied: "You will go with this gentleman there and crack a safe. Don't forget your acetylene torch and other tools."

"Well then," laughed the Pig with his spirited hoarse voice. "First things first. What's our share of the loot from the safe?"

"The contents belong to the gentleman," replied Govern. "That is, at least everything that is actually his property."

"We don't understand," growled Half-Ear. "If we crack the safe and are caught, we get ten years but no judge in England would punish this gentleman here. So I think that the thing must be worth it."

"It should be, too." confirmed the pawnbroker and turned to the banker: "How much will you give to these people for their work?"

Undecided the miserly usurer looked at the questioner.

After a prolonged pause, he finally said: "I think ten pounds will suffice."

The Pig snorted loudly, made a mocking whistle and

cried: "Sir! For ten pounds we don't even get out bed! Say a hundred pounds, and we can go work."

The banker drummed his fingers nervously on the greasy counter and could not decide to agree.

"Well, will he answer soon?" said Half-Ear. "It's drafty up here in the shop and I don't want to catch a cold."

"Well, I think," interjected Jack, "the price isn't too high. The boys risk their freedom."

"And under certain circumstances even some lead bullets," completed the Pig. "The gentleman doesn't know his business."

"Fine," agreed the banker, eventually. "I agree."

"Payment will be made now," said Half-Ear, although the banker thought they already completed negotiations.

Reluctantly the usurer pulled from his breast pocket the bank notes which the two men had demanded.

Suspiciously they held each pound note against the light and checked out their authenticity before the bills disappeared into their pockets, nodded their heads with satisfaction and growled:

"All right!"

Then they shook the usurer's hand to cement their good will and with that they left the dive.

From a lonely storage building on the Thames they got the tools that they needed to break open the safe. Then they all took a cab and drove through London to Regent Park.

When they arrived near the house, they left the car and crept up to lay in the darkness, scouting out the villa to determine the best approach to the house.

Despite their caution they did not notice that behind the garden's thick bushes two men huddled: Detective Marholm and Sergeant Tyler.

Inspector Baxter had left behind the two men and sharply ordered them to guard the house, since in his opinion the Master Thief Raffles could not have left the villa.

With great interest they watched the burglars at work.

The invaders carefully threw a rope to the mezzanine floor through which they would break in, and carried with them tools to open the safe.

The Bug rubbed his hand in pleasure and whispered to Sergeant Tyler. "We have more luck than judgment, hell yes, sergeant. We'll both be promoted tomorrow!" Then with more violent agitation he grabbed his colleague by the arm and with a low voice continued: "Goddam, Tyler, if I'm not mistaken there in the window of the villa is the same man we saw when we visited banker Gordon."

"That's impossible!"

Sergeant Tyler looked closer, but after several seconds, he nodded, "You're right, Marholm, I want to lose ten pounds to a penny if that's not James Gordon."

"Without a doubt!" whispered the detective, "and now it's clear, Sergeant Tyler, after Raffles robbed this guy, when we went to see him this afternoon he wanted nothing to do with us. He was afraid that we were on to his tricks."

"Certainly," replied Tyler, "This is clear to me."

"Well, then," laughed the Bug. "I've always thought you were smarter than you looked."

"Make no more rotten jokes!" Sergeant Tyler growled angrily. "We're not all as brilliant as Sherlock Holmes, and yet, since he's appeared in London, we detectives at Scotland Yard are asked if we can track the criminals from dust in the air."

"Not at all a bad idea," quipped Detective Marholm, "We need to alert the captain. Hupp, now why are these boys there when the safe is already empty? Pft. But listen, get to the phone, it's at the fifth lantern, counting from the corner to the top of the street, and warn Scotland Yard."

"All right, sir!" and led by the command the sergeant crept away.

A quarter of an hour passed before Tyler returned. Then they moved closer to the house and went in the same way as the criminals.

Being careful not to make any noise they climbed the stairs to where Lord Lister's study and bedroom were located.

At the very moment when they entered the antechamber, they heard a loud voice say, "Stop or I'll shoot!"

A desperate roar followed, then several shots.

They rushed forward into the study.

But in the pale light when they pushed open the door,

62

they collided with the fleeing criminals.

Detective Marholm grabbed the Pig and used jiu-jitsu to neatly throw him down to the ground, and bashed him on the temple.

Half-Ear in contrast ripped open a window and boldly jumped into space.

"Good evening, sirs," echoed to the detectives. The words came from Lord Lister, who was in his pajamas, having been in bed asleep, a revolver now in his hand. "You see, they wanted to rob me twice."

He had turned on the room's electric light. A new scene presented itself immediately: Crouching hidden in the safe was James Gordon.

Sergeant Tyler pulled him out and put him in handcuffs.

The man trembled with fear and then angrily looked at the detective and Lord Lister.

Then flashed a devilish steel of joy in his eyes. Turning to the officer and pointing to Lord Lister, he said:

"Gentlemen! You have made a good catch!"

"Certainly," laughed Marholm, who was still in high spirits after capturing the Pig. "We've been looking for this guy for a long time. He's earned at least twenty years behind bars!"

"No!" cried James Gordon, "I don't mean that, but that man there."

Pointing at Lord Lister: "There is Raffles!"

"That's completely crazy!" laughed Sergeant Tyler.

63

And Marholm said: "Now you probably want to play the wild man? No, my dear sir, look around; no one will listen."

"I beseech you, gentlemen!" wailed the handcuffed banker, all his limbs trembling, "take him prisoner. I swear to you, he's Raffles."

"Shut up," said the sergeant, "before you offend his lordship's honorable person."

At that moment in front of the home a patrol from Scotland Yard arrived.

The command had rang out, and in a few seconds the chief detective came by car to the house.

After Marholm briefly explained to Inspector Baxter what was transpiring he was ordered to bring the banker to headquarters.

The usurer once again repeated his accusation against Lord Lister and implored the inspector and the detective to hear his words.

When he finally realized that none of the officers believed him, he began to rage and curse like a madman.

Desperate, he flapped his arms around and screamed over and over again: "There is Raffles! Raffles is there!"

"Take him, boys!" commanded Baxter, "he wants to play the wild man."

Four powerful fists packed him up and managed Gordon out of the room.

The detectives followed.

Half-Ear was still in the garden, as he had broken his foot in the fall, and he laid moaning and whimpering in the bushes.

Finally as detective Marholm jumped into the patrol wagon he looked at the brightly lit windows of the upper floor at the sharp silhouette of Lord Lister and could see him standing there smoking a cigarette.

Chapter VII

At Scotland Yard

It was 10 o'clock the next morning, when a representative from the burglary and theft insurance company appeared at
Police Inspector Baxter's office, to inquire about the case of
break-in at Lord Lister's house.

"It's remarkable, Sir," he explained to the insurance
official, "this man, this Raffles, takes me and the whole world
for a fool. In front of my own eyes he stole the money."

"Incredible," said the representative, shaking his head, "I
wouldn't believe it if you didn't tell me yourself. By the way, did
you see the money that was stolen from the Lord yourself?"

"Yes," confirmed the inspector, "I saw it with my own
eyes."

"This desperate act leaves us with nothing but to pay."

"You'll definitely need to do that," Baxter said

66

approvingly.

"Then please sign for me this letter of indemnity for my company."

With these words the insurance official took from his briefcase a document which needed the inspector's signature to confirm that the amount stolen was £20,000.

Without any hesitation, Baxter signed his name.

Then the representative endorsed it.

After he left, the captain called for the arrested banker Gordon and his accomplice.

The detectives gathered in the inspector's office and the prisoner was brought in.

After gathering personal information the interrogation began.

James Gordon realized that his only salvation depended on his tricks or he faced a severe prison sentence. He was like a fox biting off his own leg to escape a trap.

So he began by telling Inspector Baxter and the detectives what induced him to carry out the burglary at Lord Lister's villa, and what had led him there, without telling them about the robbery and ambush by Raffles.

As proof he showed the detectives the letter from Lord Lister, the same one which he had also shown his business friend Govern earlier.

An immense excitement seized the listening officials. It was literally the only evidence they had against the Great

Unknown, the brilliant Raffles, even though only officers with the best arrest records could make detective in Scotland Yard.

"Why didn't you say something earlier?" cried Captain Baxter angrily at the banker. "You know that there's a £1,000 reward for the arrest of Raffles."

"I sang it to you in every key but you didn't want to believe me," said James Gordon, "more than once I told you about Lord Lister."

"It's heartbreaking!" roared to the inspector and ran like a mad man around his office, back and forth. Suddenly he pulled himself together, and ordered:

"Come on, men, we can still take a number of our best detectives. Ah, he won't escape us. We'll charge at his lordship. We will crack this nut!"

"Let's hope for the best!" Detective Marholm said. "I just think that by the time we get there the nest will be empty. It would really be a shame if he fell into our hands. He could still cause us a lot of interesting adventures. The man mocked us, but can teach us something about courage and proficiency."

Baxter yelled at him in fury:

"Shut up, you! Don't think about admiring this scoundrel. You are completely useless to the detective profession!"

"I doubt that," replied Marholm and smiled sarcastically, "A few minutes ago you were extremely flattering to me about capturing these criminals."

"Let's not waste time," said Sergeant Tyler, "we have to

try to catch Raffles."

That settled it almost immediately, and the detectives prepared to leave Scotland Yard.

When they reached the doorway Marholm remarked to Baxter: "You doubt my detective abilities, but as a detective I have a good lesson for your esteemed person. An hour ago you told the insurance company representative that Lord Lister's claim was valid. It could be of great value to them if you told them that Lord Lister is Raffles and not to pay out the claim."

"Goddam!" cried Baxter and rushed back to Scotland Yard, "You're right, I had almost forgotten. I'll ring them up at once."

Detective Marholm accompanied him to the telephone booth.

In a few seconds the connection was made, and in that moment Police Inspector Baxter learned a valuable lesson, namely that Raffles was faster than him, and that the insured sum was already paid.

The nervous captain accompanied by Marholm went out to the waiting officers and the car sped them on to Regent Park.

Lord Lister in his study was in the meantime unaware of the danger which threatened him, and was packing a big suitcase.

He had put in a few things when Charlie Brand entered.

He took off his overcoat and hat and gazed at his friend and the suitcase thoughtfully. After some time, Lord Lister said to himself, "I'm not going to pack a suitcase, it would be a

69

mistake to take it."

His secretary, on hearing these words, said, "But you'll need it on the trip, because you can't go without these things."

"Why not?" said Lister, "Such things are like ballast on a hot air balloon; the time spent worrying about them is time you should spend worrying about yourself. All over the world I can get all the money that I need, and avoid the unnecessary weight. By the way, it took you a long while to deal with the insurance company. Did they give you a hard time?"

"Not at all," replied Charlie, "but they sent one of their officials to see Inspector Baxter in Scotland Yard for more information. The captain confirmed my statements, and the company paid, with a pretty surly manner, the insured sum."

"Well," laughed Lord Lister, "the gentlemen that would rather take than spend at all have a great idea: when a company steals it isn't villainy, it's just business.

"People badly miscalculate their investments; if all men possessed the sensible idea of getting insurance against their losses the dividends of their shares would offset any theft. There is an incredible amount of money stolen. I almost like to say that there is not enough money to pay for the all the theft that occurs daily. Incidentally, where's the money?"

"It's all here," and Charlie pulled from his pocket a packet containing 20 one-thousand-pound notes.

Lord Lister took the money, counted it and carefully put it in his wallet.

An ironic smile played around his clean-cut mouth.

"Well," he said, "the deal was worth it. Now if only this unknown Raffles would actually steal a real chunk of money from me."

"A fortune," noted the secretary, "that you ought to insure it against theft."

His friend laughed and patted him on the shoulder.

"Charlie," he said, "so if you don't have anything what do you do?"

"When you have nothing," repeated Charlie, "yes, then one does not need insurance."

"Very well!" laughed Lord Lister; "This is also a perception. But yet it is not quite true. For example, I am insured in case in the future I have something stolen from me."

"Hmm..." went the other, "you always have your own philosophy and you remind me of Sherlock Holmes in that way. The main thing is that you now have enough money for a trip to Europe."

"I want to be ready," said Lord Lister. "My instinct tells me that I'm finished here, but I also still think London is a place that offers more than all the remaining cities in the world put together."

At this moment, the valet entered and announced:

"My Lord! Outside is a man, an untrustworthy looking individual. He looks like somebody you don't want to meet."

"Well, well, then it can only be a policeman," joked the

71

Lord.

"No," replied the valet, "this guy looks pretty scruffy."

"Oh, my favorite men's fashion. Is there's only one?"

"Only one," answered the valet. "but I prefer to deal with a dozen other people."

"All right! Invite him in anyway."

The valet bowed and left.

Lord Lister thought for a second and then asked Charlie:

"Please, listen, my boy, go to Victoria Station and wait for me there by the newsstand, where the trains run to the port. If I have to change my schedule, we can take the night train."

"Shouldn't I stay with you?" Charlie said. "We can go to the station together."

Lord Lister looked his fine young friend seriously in the eye and said:

"Charlie, do you remember how you came to me six months ago? And after we knew each other two days, you told me that if you didn't get help you would eat a bullet? I took your gun away from you for safety and made you realize that debts of honor and all other debts are as reckless as gambling debts, and it doesn't matter that the gentlemen who had played you wore a tuxedo and tails and is one of the state-protected dark men. I proved to you then that a human life is a precious thing, and that you can realize this only when you hit rock bottom. All of these explanations which I gave you caused you to serve me like an I'm an older and more experienced friend. But you're only a few years younger than me, and I think that after half a year by my side you find yourself a tested and qualified comrade and therefore I will have no secrets from you."

He smoked a few puffs from his cigarette and continued:

"Look, Charlie, the money which I gave you for support as a gentleman has helped me personally as well, along with all the disinherited, unfortunate and disposable people needing welfare whom I meet. They are underused assets, and I have learned much from them."

Lord Lister stood silent and smoked a new cigarette, while he watched Charlie nervously and with keen interest.

"I don't understand you completely," he said after a pause, "you said, Edward, you earn a fortune with your brain. But I've never I seen you but either working or exert any such activity. Will you tell me how you obtained such wealth?"

"Oh, yes," replied his friend and flicked the ash from in a wide arc. Then he looked again at Charlie's eyes, and immediately replied:

"John Raffles!"

The young man stared at him, as if he had seen a ghost.

"Are you playing another a joke on me, Edward?" he asked in disbelief and embarrassment.

"Not at all," said Lord Lister, "A year ago I became Raffles to balance the wealthy and starving classes."

"You're really him?" Charlie asked, and there was still doubt in his face.

"My word of honor!" confirmed Lord Lister. "I am Raffles."

"But how could you...I can hardly grasp it. It sounds like a fairy tale...how did this happen?"

"Very simple," was the reply, "My father and mother lost their entire fortune to one of these criminal stock jobbers from London; I spent my youth in the deepest misery. My father took his own life while this scoundrel still rides in our parks as a gentleman with four horses and has a castle in Scotland. He has built all his wealth on a bogus fortune. The law would take no action against the villain.

"I realized in my rags that there existed a large horde of stock exchange bandits and other riff-raff. Hundreds of thousands of people have to indulge in daily drudgery to pay for their lavish lifestyles.

"Of these, the poor made but a meager living, while these parasites live in the lap of luxury, the best life can offer.

"Since then I have taken a narrow path through large crowds to fight against this breed and take from them the wealth they have looted from the masses and give it back to them. And now I ask you, Charlie, do you want to help me in this fight? Or not don't be afraid to tell me. Say it frankly. You know I love openness."

Without hesitation, the young gentleman took his friend's right hand and held it firmly and insisted:

"Yes, Edward!" I have your back! Whatever it may be, I

will be by your side and do everything I can for you."

"All right!" The Lord nodded, "I knew it. Now Listen:

"On the way to Victoria Station when you pass the Salvation Army, put in an anonymous donation of £5,000."

He took from his breast pocket the money he received and handed it to him. "Furthermore," he continued, "Take £5,000 and give it to the Bureau of Orphans from the rest of the money. Don't use my name anywhere. I want no more than a receipt. Now go, my boy, and wait for me...as I told you."

Charlie put the money in his portfolio; both shook hands again, and the master thief's new assistant left the room.

A few moments later Lord Lister rang for his valet and told him to bring in his waiting guest.

Immediately entered a much neglected-subject. Without waiting for an invitation, the unknown visitor sat in a chair and began to fill his pipe with shag tobacco, and to smoke it.

After a few puffs he cleared his throat and spat in an uninhibited way on the barren, expensive carpet.

Lord Lister watched him with his hands in his pockets.

"You are not at home, my friend," he finally spoke to the stranger "and this isn't a pub in East End or Whitechapel."

"I know," said the stranger in a short, husky and brandy voice.

"Yeah," said Lord Lister, "then I'm surprised that you confuse my carpet with the pavement. So what leads you here?"

"Business," was the terse response.

"Business?" John Raffles repeated, "I don't have any business with you."

"You will. Listen to me: I would be Tom Pitt and down out in the East Street I'm known as a man that in a flash can put a knife between your third and fourth ribs. That's just a taste of my agility. Do you want to know more?"

He jumped up and put his right hand into his pocket, as if he wanted to pull it out a knife.

Lord Lister stood motionless.

"I have no business with you," he said dismissively.

"Not so," replied the stranger and then in turn. "I just wanted to introduce myself."

"So you know me already?" asked the Lord suddenly.

The stranger looked at him puzzled and replied:

"Me? No, try again."

Lister laughed. "It's not a joke but you look like you've done a few years."

"Well, if you already know, don't ask me about it; but I wasn't guilty. Goddam, it could happen to anybody! I'm as pure as a child under the sun. There was nothing you could show me."

"Yeah, that would be right, and now explain to me quickly what you want with me."

"Hmm...," said the stranger, "I'll tell you briefly: the other night I went to an old haunt, a storage building in Tower Street and stayed there. When I got up a few hours ago I noticed that some men came in and under all kinds of junk they took

76

some housebreaking tools. I heard those people mention your name."

"So then, you want to notify me some people intend to break into my house? And you want to get paid for your warning? I'll give you a ten-pound note."

The smoking intruder was allowed to continue and spat before he closed his mouth again, and continued:

"I'm not here for a ten pound note, it's a whole other thing that led me here, and I believe that you are worth at least £5,000 for my other communications concerning your own person."

The lord laughed, amused, without returning a word.

"I think," continued the stranger, "that someone as rich as you will happily pay £5,000 for a message which is worth £50,000. I also think you'll have to talk to me when I tell you that I know things about a certain Raffles, you..."

"Your remarks barely interest me," was the calm reply. "I don't pay spies. If this is why you came, you can leave the room right now."

The rough man stood up, knocked his pipe in his ashtray, slipped it into his pocket and pulled out a bottle of brandy.

Smacking he lips he put the opening to his mouth and took a long drink, then offered it to Lord Lister, who fended it off with a gesture and said, "Drink your brandy alone; I usually drink my own."

Thus, the uninvited visitors closed the bottle and put it in his shirt; then he muttered:

"You're not a gentleman if you refuse to drink with a colleague."

Lord Lister laughed again; the rotten scoundrel's naiveté amused him.

"A nice camaraderie," he replied, "but I'd also like to do without it."

The eyes of his opponent flashed malicious hatred. He realized that he was no match for John Raffles, and saw that he was being ridiculed.

"Goddam!" he swore, "the devil take you fine scoundrels! The devil take me, too, if you could bluff me. You may be able to impress your servant in kid gloves and tailcoat but not me. Now I ask you for the last time: will you give me £5,000 or not?"

Lord Lister shot him a short glance, raised his hand to the door gruffly, "No!"

"All right!" replied the stranger, "then we'll have to speak a different language."

In a flash he tore a broad dagger from the side pocket of his coat and jumped tiger-like at Raffles.

The attack had been expected.

With a rapid arm swing he parried the knife of the shocked assassin, and in one movement grabbed him by the shirt and with a jiu-jitsu trick ripped his jacket down on both sides over his upper arms, so that the man stood defenseless.

In a moment the Lord jumped like a spring to the open door and threw him into the hallway.

Cursing and swearing the crook hastened down the stairs and out of the house.

Lord Lister rang for his valet: "Listen, Fred," he said quietly, "I'll be traveling for a long time and ask that during my absence you keep up the house until I send you any new orders."

"Very good," replied the servant, bowing, "does your lordship want me to pack his case?"

"No, thank you, I travel without baggage."

Fred bowed again, and then came the front doorbell.

Both listened a moment, and the valet then asked: "Is your lordship receiving visitors?"

"Yes," replied his master, and Fred left the room to open the front door.

After a few minutes, Miss Walton came in with a big bouquet of flowers.

Astonished, Lord Lister looked at her.

"Forgive me for coming to you, my Lord," said the young woman with her sweet voice, "I just wanted to present you some flowers as a thank you from my mother and me before you leave."

She offered to him with a joyful smile a magnificent bouquet.

"Flowers?" John Raffles stirred, "they are for me the most beautiful thing I know in the world."

"Oh, I love them too much," said Walton Miss confused.

"A flower," continued Lord Lister, "always reminds me of a beautiful woman." He looked at her charming, blushing face and her dark eyes.

He forgot completely that he was about to leave his house, and that with each second he was in danger about which his instinct already warned him.

He politely escorted Miss Walton to sit in front of the fireplace.

"I wanted to spend time with you tonight," said the young lady hesitantly, "I see that you packing your bags, and I don't wish to disturb you. Ah, travel must be wonderful! Since I was young I wanted to take a long trip, possibly to the south of Italy."

"Were you never out of London?" Raffles engaged.

"No, never. To my shame, I must confess that I still am an Englander; I have never even seen the ocean. We were too poor, sir."

"What was your father, if I may ask?"

"A sailor, a naval officer. He died after an accident at sea. Oh, we can't even maintain his grave; it's at the bottom of the ocean. My mother received a small pension, but after a year of illness we have pawned everything; now we have nothing."

"And your relative, this police inspector Baxter, he knows your plight exactly?"

"Very well" said Miss Walton, "he acts as our

80

pawnbroker."

"A cute cousin!" He convulsed as the words came out. "How is he related to you?"

"He is my mother's half-brother. I told you already what a hard-hearted man he is."

"It is no worse or better than all the English; I hope I can show him a little receipt for what he did to you."

At this moment there was a knock at the door.

The old servant came and reported:

"Excuse me, your Lordship, the police officers who were here earlier tonight have come again."

Lord Lister thought for a moment, took a cigarette, smoked it and laughed easily.

"I believe," he said, "the gentlemen must have forgotten something in this house."

"Has they forgotten something?" Fred repeated amazed and looked searchingly around the room.

"Yes, my old friend," laughed Raffles, "namely, they have forgotten to take the rascal they seek."

"Yes—could he be still here?" The man made a silly face and looked around the room again.

The Lord laughed and slapped him on the shoulder, saying in a confidential manner:

"He's still here, Fred, but I think tonight that they'll be able to catch him."

Then he went to the window and looked out onto the

street.

He whistled. He saw probably a dozen uninformed policeman who were not going to just charge the house.

"Your fox hunt is on," he murmured to himself; "Well then, let them try their best."

Then he turned again to the servant:

"Listen carefully, Fred, to what I'm saying. The lady is my secretary if you should be so prompted; this lady, should they ask, is planning a long journey, her suitcase is there and with it Miss Walton will leave the house. Call for a car to bring her along with her luggage to the train station."

"Now tell the police officers that I have a short meeting with my secretary and that they have to be patient for a minute."

"Very well, your lordship," said deeply constructed verbs, and Fred left the room.

No sooner had the door closed when Lord Lister turned to Miss Walton, took her hands protectively and said in a low voice:

"The time has come, Miss Helen, where you can help me. I have captured from the usurer James Gordon, where your mother inquired in vain for a loan, the usurious notes which had become this bane of many unfortunate people. The man has given me up to the police; I gave him a good lesson and helped many by freeing them from the hands of this vampire."

The eyes of the young lady shone joyously, and she replied:

"You're a noble man, Lord Lister and you've helped me and my mother me with your generous service. Whatever it is, I consider myself happy if I can help you."

"It will take all your self-control, Miss Helen," said Lister further, "if you make a small mistake I'm lost."

"No, no!" replied the young woman stubbornly, "you can rely entirely on me, just tell me what I should do. Believe me, women are allied for good."

The peer took her right hand and kissed it.

In that moment, there was another knock at the door, and a gruff voice which he recognized as that of Inspector Baxter, cried out:

"Open up in the names of the law, Lord Edward Lister!"

"Right away! Just a moment!" replied the callee as he leaned over to Miss Walton and whispered:

"There is a case that is large enough to conceal me, I'll hide it and use it to escape. You will bring the luggage to Victoria Station and leave it there in a secluded space. Then we'll meet again.

"Take this money and pay for anything you need. If the policemen ask, you say that you are going away, and that this case belongs to you. Do you understand me, Miss Walton?"

"Yes," she replied, trembling, but determined. John Raffles watched as the excitement of the upcoming adventure overlaid her fresh face with a nervous pallor.

"Be strong!" he whispered.

"I am!" she replied and felt, and drew herself up proudly.

As soon as she had said these words, Lord Lister hastily rushed to the case. But before he could even open it the door of the room was thrown wide by Police Inspector Baxter, Sergeant Tyler, Inspector Marholm and two detectives.

Lister remained in spite of the great danger the master of his domain.

With his friendliest face he sneered:

"Good day, gentlemen! To what do I owe the honor of your visit? Is Raffles going to rob me again?"

"No," rejoined Baxter, "Raffles will never steal anything again, because I tell you he's arrested."

"Well," laughed the unmasked man, "but, just tell me one simple thing: explain how Raffles is arrested without you having caught him?"

"We have caught him," said Baxter.

"This is quite gratifying and I congratulate you," was the ironically polite reply.

"Yes," came from the lips of the police chief, "very encouraging, and now I urge you, Lord Lister aka Raffles, surrender. In the names of the law, I declare you under arrest."

Lord Lister with his big eyes looked at the police inspector for several seconds, and then said:

"This is an excellent joke, if you have any more in stock, I advise you to become editor of a humor magazine."

"Sir!" roared Baxter, while Detective Marholm could not

suppress a laugh. "You have fooled us long enough; now once again, I urge you to surrender!"

Lord Lister leaned against the fireplace leisurely in his bold manner, without any sign of nervousness, blew some big smoke rings from his cigarette and said with a binding laugh to Baxter, as if he was a very pleasant guest:

"I pity you, Inspector Baxter!"

"How's that?" he sneered.

"I mean," replied the questionee, "that you have the misfortune to have to deal with me."

"It will fortunately not take too long. Today after many years it is over."

And red with anger over Raffles's indifferent attitude he said to his officers:

"Let's make short work of this. Grab him!"

"Stop!" cried the Lord. "First, you must to allow this lady, who is my secretary and is about to travel to the lake for recuperation, to leave the house. That suitcase there belongs to her."

Baxter looked hesitantly at Miss Walton and realized now who she was.

"What are you doing here in this cave of thieves?" he shouted to his niece.

"Earning a living for me and mother," said Miss Walton proudly.

"A lovely bakery," grumbled the inspector. "But I can

85

see through this crook's beautiful mask."

"Rogue" thundered the voice of the Lord Lister to the police chief. "Get out of my house!"

He reached with his right hand into his breast pocket and quickly pulled out a silver receptacle.

"Look at this case, inspector. Good Petersburg friends—nihilists, you know—gave it to me to use as a last resort. This is a pocket bomb filled with dynamite, and always primed for use. Now together we will begin a great journey from which there is no return. You did not catch Raffles, Mr. Inspector, but Raffles has caught you!"

In the next moment he raised his hand to hurl the bomb at the officials.

Prior to this gesture the detectives ducked, but at the moment when they observed his raised his arm to throw it, they shook off their sluggishness and with a cry of horror fled out of the room without looking back.

"Save yourself if you can," roared Baxter.

Quick as lightning flew the silver case to the carpet and it sprung open, revealing that it was just a cigarette case.

Outside rang alarms, and whistles and confusion reigned.

Lord Lister turned to Miss Walton, posted a volatile kiss on her pure forehead and said:

"Now, Miss Helen, my fate is in your hands! Do everything I said to you."

Then he opened his suitcase, jumped in, and closed the

lid so that it appeared untouched.

A few seconds passed, then the door was carefully opened, and through the gap Inspector Marholm looked into the room.

Momentarily he opened it wide, looked around, saw the cigarette case, laughed and bent down. He picked up the cigarettes and the box and called out to the stairs:

"Inspector Baxter, come in! The dynamite was a dud. He's fooled us all again. It wasn't a pocket bomb, just a cigarette case."

The inspector and the remaining detectives with revolvers in their hands entered the study to find the Bug sitting in a chair and convulsing with laughter.

Baxter raged like a wounded boar. He ordered his officers to search the whole house.

"The villain cannot have escaped!" he cried, "He can't be gone, he has to sit in this accursed Burrow, and I'm not leaving this house until I have discovered his secret hideout behind the wall!"

Enraged, he tapped his fingers on the lid of the case.

Now he turned to Miss Walton, and asked her:

"Which way did he go?"

Miss Walton replied, "I don't know. I think he's gone through that room." Then she added: "I want to leave with my mother on the noon train and it won't wait so I don't want to continue to have any difficulty here, please."

Then she called the valet and together they moved the heavy suitcase, which the inspector assumed belonged to her, out of the room.

Detective Marholm, who saw the young lady struggling with her baggage summoned some allies to help, and ordered into the house some standing policemen and ordered:

"Carry the lady's suitcase to the car."

Miss Walton thanked him with a charming smile, and while the police officers carried the bag down the stairs in front of her, she sighed with relief and she felt as if the sky reflected the heavy burden of her heart.

It was echoed by the raging and ranting of the Raffles-seeking police captain.

He knocked on the walls, expecting to find a secret door and got himself a ladder to investigate the ceiling itself...

Unencumbered by this Miss Walton and her suitcase got into the car and drove straight to Victoria Station.

There, she let them bring the luggage into a secluded room and told the porters that she needed to repack some things.

As soon as she was alone in the room, she opened the suitcase, and a well-kept Lord Lister, alias John Raffles, jumped out.

He extended his cramped right hand, the result of his uncomfortable body position. Then he turned to Miss Walton, kissed her two hands and said with a warm glow in his eyes:

"You're a brave girl, Miss Helen. I am eternally grateful.

If I did not find myself on the run, I wanted to see if it was possible for me to win more than your friendship. I hope that I will return within a short time without suffering their judgment."

Miss Walton lowered her blushing head, since she was unable to grasp why that the noble, proud man himself competed for her favor.

Once again Raffles seized Miss Walton's hands and kissed them. Then he whispered a faint: "God bless! Don't forget to say hello to your mother and don't you forget about me. I hope to see you soon!"

Then he hurriedly left the room.

On the platform for the Queesborough train he met Charlie Brand.

"It's high time!" cried the secretary, "the train leaves in five minutes."

"All right, Charlie," said Raffles. "I just need to stop by the telegraph station."

Once there, he sent a telegram to his valet.

This done, he said to Charlie:

"I've been thinking about staying in London. I intend to rent a small country estate in the West End for a while."

He disappeared with his friends into the bustling crowd.

Baxter summoned some craftsmen to the floor of the study and had ripped open a wall, while detective Marholm examined the bedroom on his own.

After closing the sliding door between the two rooms he

went into the bathroom, and discovered in the wall there an opening through which one could get to the grandfather clock in the study.

Baxter heard the noise which Marholm made behind the clock. He listened with sharp ears, and a triumphant smile flew over his face.

"The mouse is caught in the trap," he said to himself and waved to the officers to follow him: "We've got him!" he whispered to the detectives, "I've discovered his spider hole. He's there in the clock!"

Noiselessly as possible, the officers stood at the big timepiece as Detective Marholm opened the door from the inside. Unknowingly, he stepped out. A dozen fists caught him somewhat roughly on the shoulders and arms.

"Are you crazy?" Marholm cried and tried to shake the detectives off him.

"Stop him. Stop him!" cried Baxter, who was so blinded by rage and his burning desire to catch the Great Unknown, even blindly, he pulled away his subordinates without recognizing him.

But the policemen saw their mistake and let their colleague free.

Marholm rubbed his aching body from their powerful fists, and started to laugh at Baxter, who looked at him with an infinitely stupid, bewildered face.

Before he could say anything, the fugitive's valet entered

and handed the police inspector a telegram.

He took it and read:

"POLICE INSPECTOR BAXTER I CONGRATULATE
YOU ON YOUR SUCCESS
"JOHN C RAFFLES"

While the chief threw a temper tantrum, Marholm left
the room and laughed harder than he ever laughed in his life.

THE END

COVER

GALLERY

Lord Lister

genannt

Raffles

der

Lister

Meisterdieb

3. Band — Der Ordensraub im Königsschlosse. — 20 Pf 25 Heller 25 Cts

„Hallo, Kapitän Baxter, wohin soll die Reise gehen?" lachte John Raffles, die Hand vom Druckknopf nehmend.

19. Band   Das Erbe vom Eaglestone.   **20 Pf.** 25 Heller 25 Cts.

Im schnellen Wurf schüttete der Falschmünzer das glühende Metall auf seinen Gegner.

Lord genannt der grosse Lister Raffles Unbekannte

20. Band — Der rote Meister. — 20 Pf. 25 Heller 50 Cts.

Noch einen Augenblick, dann mußte das Rasiermesser den Strick zerschneiden und die Bombe im Fall zur Explosion bringen.

50. Bind — Solgudens Præst — 25 Øre

Den tatoverede Præst dansede oppe paa Azteker-Altret, mens han svingede med Guldøksen.

Número 1 — El tesoro en un sarcófago — 25 cénts.

El traqueteo del tren impidió que se oyese el ruido que hacía lord Lister trabajando debajo del vagón.

Bind: 25 Øre. 30. Juni 1928

Indbrudet i Sovevognen.

Over dem laa Den kvindelige Detektiv, mens Lord Lister tilegnede sig Nøglen fra den sovende Dame.

193. Bind   Hvert Bind indeholder en afsluttet Fortælling   50 Øre

LORD LISTER

GENTLEMAN - TYVEN -

Det forbandede Guld

»Nu kan du omkomme paa den øde Ø,« sagde Kaptajnen haanligt.

100

LORD LISTER

GENAAMD RAFFLES
NIEUWE AVONTUREN

DE GROTE ONBEKENDE

DE SCHAT OP DE ZEEBODEM

WEKELIJKSE AFLEVERING

45 Ct
N° 2800

LORD LISTERs Bedrifter

PRIS 25 ØRE

I Spilledjævelens Klør. | Nr. 14

Coming soon:

The Witch Hunter's Wards

Joseph A. Lovece is a retired journalist, and collector of dime novels, pulp magazines and comic books. He lives in Ormond Beach, Florida.

Printed in Great Britain
by Amazon

32515495R00066